A BRIGHT
BLUE PEBBLE
And other stories

An Almost Book

Mike Williamson

ISBN:198163021X
ISBN-13:9781981630219

CONTENTS

FOREWORD

It is a fact that in the future something momentous will happen; it may be tonight, or a billion years from now, but it will cause us to leave our planet one way or the other. In five billion years, the Sun will expand and then die, and without it, nothing can live. It sounds like a long time, five billion, but that is just the deadline, literally, and a meteor could hit us tonight, or we could kill the planet and all that exists on it, and we   have   done   nothing   about   it

A BRIGHT
BLUE PEBBLE

The journey had started long ago with a single thought when it was realised that they had to move on, the thought became a word, and then a shout that echoed through eternity. Some argued hopefully that things would improve with time, and so the endless debates continued for generations until even the most stubborn resistance had to agree to the facts – their world was dying.

They had left it almost too late; the endless bickering had gone on for too many generations! The thoughtless extravagance that had been characteristic of the earlier times meant that raw materials had almost vanished, billions of tons of copper and mint coloured earth, transformed into ploughshares and swords, and that would make it difficult to produce the vast ship, but by creating new types of material and ravishing the last of the raw material from the soil, the ship was finally waiting for them.

It hovered over the planet, quietly murmuring to

itself in strange words as it bobbed on the gravitational surf, patient and waiting. When they had designed the ship, there had been multitudes of people involved over many generations, but as the resources of the planet had diminished, the population had also reduced, some from starvation and others from uncontrollable diseases but mostly from old age. Now, when all of the remainders of people had boarded, the colossal structure would be almost empty and echoing like a huge cathedral – or an empty world.

Jon Demeri stood looking at the huge expanse of fields, growing more golden crops than their tiny population now required. He thought that it was ironic that if they had been growing these crops on the ship earlier while some had starved on the planet below, it would have eased their lives; now there was plenty for everyone!

The automatons tended to the ripening fields and orchards, as they had done for countless years on the planet. Without the aid of these machines, they would never have built the ship or mined the materials. None of them was humanoid, just shaped for their function, so they were all shapes and sizes and some were invisible, just programmes in the aether, drifting like ghosts. They ran the ship's engines, environmental equipment, and food production, even the navigation, leaving little for the people to do except think and plan – and dream.

Tomorrow they would leave orbit in search of a new home, where that would be, and when, nobody could guess. Here, in the inner part of the galaxy, there were more bright stars than anyone thought possible, and they were close together forming an intense ball of light around a dark nucleus. These were not the ship's destination as the life of these stars was considerably shorter than those remote stars on the galaxy's outer rim.

"What are you thinking?" Tod Rinwop came and stood beside him. Their fathers and grandfathers and great-grandfathers had worked on the original ship's design, they had all shared in the triumphs and disappointments, and there had been many of those.

"Now that we are at a point that we dreamed of for years, it all does seem like a dream," Jon replied.

"Have you looked at the planet?" Tod asked.

Jon nodded, "It is enough to make one weep! From up here, we can see the damage that we have done to our home, and I feel angry!" From space, the planet was scarred and wrinkled like a brown burnt piece of coal.

"Me too, but we are all responsible for that, even if we were not all born at the time," Tod said, "The last damage was to make this ship, and that was necessary."

"Is everyone here now?" Jon changed the subject.

"Yes, everyone except those that did not want to make the journey," Tod paused, "I can appreciate their feelings; we are on a journey to somewhere that we do not really belong, and it is comforting to be surrounded by familiar places and objects. It is a stuff of dreams and memories."

"What do the chiefs have to say?"

Tod shrugged, "The usual stuff, half-truths or complete lies. They are painting a rosy picture of our future based on imagination, fantasy. They have nothing to say about those we leave behind."

"It may be a wreck of a planet, but I also have a longing to stay," Jon admitted, "but tomorrow we leave and we must concentrate our minds on that and the future."

The Great Ship slowly left orbit the following day; the engines hardly increased their murmur as it set out for an unknown future. Everyone sought a view of the receding planet, many were wiping away tears and comforting each other, but eventually, the husk of the planet became difficult to discern, and all turned their thoughts towards tomorrow.

***

Eved Demeri watched the instruments and listened

to the quiet readout. She was a distant descendant of Jon who left their home planet so very long ago. Suns and planets had passed by their detectors, and always there was something not quite right; too near the sun, too far from the sun, gravity too low and no water, gravity too high and they would be crushed, noxious gases or no atmosphere, whatever they saw was unsuitable.

She did not have to be looking at the results of the latest planet, but she had a feeling that soon there would be a perfect sphere, a new world beckoning for them; there must be after so long in the search. She had never stood on a planet, nor had her parents and grandparents, and she imagined what it would be like to feel warm summer breezes and cool gentle rains. Many called it freedom as though the ship was a prison.

With a sigh she turned away; this planet was too young and still very volcanic, the primitive start for a promising home. If they came back in a billion years or so, perhaps it would be a possibility.

***

With excitement, Brin Demeri turned on the viewer. He was the latest in the long line of descendants of the family Demeri. His forbear Jon had by now assumed the stature of a mythical patriarch, and as a young boy, Brin was introduced to the place where everyone's ashes were deposited; it was a colossal sombre monument. The names formed a legend.

Today was a great day; at least he could feel it coursing through his veins, prickling and thumping as he double checked the instruments. The readout was confirmed in a gentle tone that this planet could be just what they had been looking for!

He had sounded the alarm, and everyone came to witness the new discovery; those that could not find the room near the controls found a viewer somewhere else. There was a collective sigh as the sensor depicted a distant spot of light, and as they drew closer, it took the form of a bright blue pebble.

"Ahh!" they all sighed. "Water!" said the readout, and they sighed again. "Breathable air!" and they sighed again. "Gravity, one gee!" and they started crying.

The dreams of a million lifetimes had come true; here was a beautiful planet with deep blue oceans and wide continents, tall mountains to climb and green trees to welcome them home.

THE SELENE ORCHID

Marni Frome was in love! Not a very surprising situation for a nineteen-year-old! He had met Rista Demeri four days earlier at a small festive gathering of friends. To him, she was a blonde vision of heaven, and she laughed at his jokes and danced divinely.

He had just spent a delightful evening with her and their friends, and now he was walking on air home along the country road, lost in thoughts of his romance and oblivious of where his feet were taking him. At the moment, those feet were taking him into the Twilight Forest.

There was no danger for him, as all of the doubtful and dangerous creatures had been removed and replaced with their own collection of animals and plants from the gene bank; in any case, he had walked this path many times during the day and night without problems.

His wandering feet whispered over the sandy surface, alongside the shy violets and glowing primrose. He stopped to admire a group of long stems that were yet to flower, their buds bursting through the green covers.

That reminded him of her emerald eyes, flashing like come-hither beacons, burning and cool at the same time. Her hair was like summer straw, but soft and flowing like the wind.

The first thing that broke into his reverie was the aroma, not quite sweet with a hint of musk, almost a woman's perfume. He had never experienced this smell in the countryside or woods before, at least not when he was alone. His feet carried him further into the forest, the aroma increased in strength, it was enticing but not overpowering.

As he walked on, the scent appeared to be stronger to the right, taking him off the path and deeper and darker into the midnight shadows of the wood. The shadows became more intense so that he had to feel his way from tree to tree until finally, he saw that there was a spot just ahead that was showing a soft luminance and outlining the trees.

There was a small clearing, in the centre of which was a single huge exotic white and pink flower-bloom larger than his head and the luminescence was coming from its large but delicate petals.

"It is an orchid, a Selene Orchid." A strange voice came from the shadows.

Marni peered into the hidden corners, and then he saw what appeared to be a pair of dark shining eyes like whirling rainbows looking at him. As his eyes adjusted, he saw that the eyes belonged to a peculiar creature; dark eyes in a green animal squatting on the far side of the orchid.

"It is a special flower that only appears occasionally," the creature said, "I am its Graken."

"What is a Graken?" Marni asked.

"Its protector," the Graken replied.

"It is very beautiful," Marni said, breathing in the delightful scent "but why Selene?"

"Because the light comes from the Lover of the Night!" Graken answered.

"What is the Lover of the Night?"

"Selene is the Goddess of Love," Graken said from his wide mouth, "It is the soft light that shines on those in love as they walk hand in hand under her influence."

Marni looked up and saw that the Moon was indeed shining through the tree branches, "Is that Selene?"

"She has many names and sometimes it is a he, or just is," Graken hopped forward, and Marni realised that it was a huge frog.

"I have never had a frog talk to me before," Marni

said. The flower's scent was making everything slightly out of focus, in sound as well as sight, but he did not feel alarmed at this strange meeting.

"I am not a frog, I am a Graken! Do you talk to animals? Then why shouldn't animals talk to you?" Graken wiped his mouth with a webbed paw.

"No reason I suppose," Marni gave a short laugh, "I never thought of it that way."

"We are not all that different, you and I," Graken hopped nearer, "We feel and fear just like you, we hunger and love, and seek those that are attractive, and you are in love!"

"Am I?" Marni identified and admitted to himself the euphoric feeling that he had, "I suppose that I am, but what is the orchid to do with that?"

"The Selene Orchid only appears to those that are truly in love," Graken explained, "Look deep into the blossom and tell me what you see."

Marni leaned forward, looked past the ivory light of the petals and past the honeyed stamen, breathing in the honey sweetness that made him so weak at the knees and when the dizziness stopped, he saw the world and all that lived there, and he finally understood.

SUMMER HAZE

Celn lifted the latch and stepped into the henhouse. Her small hands took the almost liquid seed and poured it into the container like golden water, and the birds hungrily pecked away at it. Her costume was a pair of dungarees, reasonably clean at the moment, but by the end of the day, they would most likely be soiled from sitting on the ground, crawling through hedges or riding the pony. Occasionally, there would be a tear to be mended or a button to be replaced. For all of that, she was considered a reasonably good child.

From the house came the smells, the morning smells of freshly baked rolls and the mouth-watering smell of bacon sizzling under the grill. Her brother Perd was just now fetching a pail of fresh milk from the dairy, and her young tongue could already taste the warm and almost chewy liquid. Their cows produced the creamiest milk in the county!

Her mother called out in her musical voice, like a bell chiming, and Grandpapa answered in his deep, gruff bass. Soon, her father would appear to wash his hands and join them at the breakfast table, his tenor laughter complimenting the other instruments. Granmama's small voice whispered in the background like a soft clarinet. The family was a small orchestra!

A duck waddled hopefully after Celn as she crossed the yard and climbed the porch, pecking at the wooden clogs that Grandpapa had made a month earlier.

"That is the last of the sowing until next year," her father sang out as he sat down and helped himself to a bread roll.

"They reckon that it will be a hot summer," rumbled Grandpapa like a kettle-drum, "We will have to use the water-cart more often."

"They have never got the forecast right," Mother's voice chimed out, "so don't fret as yet!"

"Next week, there will be a meeting of the council…" Father began to say.

"Lot of idiots!" Grandpapa trumpeted, "They know nothing about farming!"

"Perhaps that is true," her Father said good-naturedly, "They are going to announce which machines we get for the harvest."

Celn fidgeted on her chair. She was just tall enough to sit at the table without the high-chair, and she listened as the others discussed the hardly understood matters. She spread sweet golden honey on a thick brown open roll and took a big bite, smearing some on her freckled nose. Mother leaned over and wiped off the honey.

With breakfast consumed and the conversation over for the time being, Father went out to tend to the chores, Mother washed the dishes and she and Granmama started preparing for their lunch, their voices chiming like a choir. Grandpapa filled his pipe with sweet tobacco and settled down in his large armchair to read a book, something he did every morning after breakfast, and in the afternoon after lunch.

Celn was fascinated at the strange markings on the pages and snuggled on Grandpapa's lap to find out what they were. Next year she would go with Perd to the school and learn how to read and write, and what numbers meant. In the meantime, she fell asleep on the old man's lap until he rose to help himself to the fresh coffee on the stove.

He settled down again, and laying the book aside, he told Celn stories of knights in armour and maidens being rescued, with Granmama tut-tutting in the background, "You're filling the poor girl's head full of nonsense!"

"It is history, Ginny," he replied, using his pet name for his wife "The real nonsense is in that school!"

Ginny punched the dough angrily; he always said that the school was not good, and she had little schooling in her childhood to know different.

Grandpapa smiled and continued with the stories, some remembered from books read long ago, others pieced together from various sources and the rest were made up.

Mother produced a plate of sweet cinnamon biscuits for everyone and a glass of creamy milk for Celn. After finishing that, Celn went out in the yard to see what was happening. The dog Char was eyeing the duck with mischievous intent; there was an eternal battle between these two as to who was the boss of the farm. Seeing Celn, the dog shook himself to change his attention and came over to her, and then followed her as she went down to the fields.

Over the pond, dragonflies darted between the reeds, bright shimmering drops of rainbows moving like lightning. On the old willow, a kingfisher sat between patrolling the pond and the stream, flashing down like a pallet of colour to the water at the slightest hint of movement.

Celn climbed the wooden fence and sat looking over the field that was displaying the green stalks of wheat. Even this early in the year, there was a shimmer over the fields, distorting the air and creating a slight haze. She took a deep breath and smelled the growing, slightly moist and tickling. It tasted powerful.

She understood the farm and the animals, thanks to Grandpapa's stories about talking rabbits, bears, and creatures living on a stream. In her mind she saw them rowing on the water and painting the doors to their homes. One half of her knew that they did not exist, and the other half wished that they did.

She did not answer for the dinner call, and Grandpapa went and found her sleeping with Char, all huddled together under the fence; she had made a daisy-chain and placed it on Char's neck. Gently he picked her up and carried her to the house, and then gently coaxed her to wakefulness.

"Oh Grandpapa!" she rubbed her still sleepy eyes, "There was such a commotion by the willow, the Vole wanted to go sailing, but Rabbit said that they should use the oars as there was no wind."

"And what did Badger say?" he asked.

"He wasn't there; I think that he had gone to see Toad." Then she smiled, happy at the thought that this old man that smelled of sweet tobacco and old words believed her, to join in the dreamland that shone in the haze of the summer mind.

THE CRYSTAL LAND

The team of five looked out from their craft over the uninviting landscape. Veleri Rinwop laid down his surveying instrument and shook his red head.

"Nothing! Absolutely nothing," he turned to the others, "I think that this is the most desolate place on the planet!"

"Maybe, and maybe not!" Tegth Demeri said, "I was on the Central Desert Expedition last year, and it looked just the same, just endless sand dunes as far as we could see, but when we investigated, it was full of amazing life forms."

"That was dry and hot," Veleri reminded him, "This is frozen water and with very intimidating low temperatures. We have proved in the lab that life forms struggle and fail at low temperatures."

"I think that we may be surprised!" Tegth continued smiling.

"They thought that of the seas," small Resta Florens piped up, "and when we looked at the deep ocean floor, we saw creatures surviving at incredible pressures and temperatures." Resta was the last member of the team with any exploration experience, and she had seen the ocean depths, with its beautiful mysteries.

"I agree with Veleri," Jib Nanth said. He was one of the technicians on the expedition; the other was Ramwe Desof who sided with Jib.

"In the desert, there can be shelter found from the heat underground," Jib continued, "but this intense cold permeates deep under the surface. I cannot believe anything can avoid the cold."

The ship that had brought them to this inhospitable place was an automaton, and the mechanical mind had selected the place and driven the prow as far into the icy shore as possible. The land vehicle was only partly an automaton, as the crew would decide on the course of the expedition.

The ramp was lowered, and the tracked vehicle crunched its way onto the frozen surface; the ship would stay, and hummed and bubbled as it waited for their return as only a patient machine can.

The snow and ice were blindingly bright in the sunshine, and the few shadows were an ethereal blue. Despite the tracks, the vehicle stumbled and slid for much of the time, the electronic brain fighting to remain on course, and then it arrived at a deep chasm. They got out and peered into the blue-green shadows far below.

"It is too wide to cross," Veleri said in his protective helmet," and I cannot see the bottom."

"We will have to travel along its length," Tegth said, "Of course, it could get wider."

Veleri snorted, "Thanks for the optimism!" and as he turned away, the once apparently firm snow gave way, and he disappeared in a waving of arms and legs in a cloud of snow. He managed to dig his gloved hands and boots into the vertical surface that produced a snow-storm, but he kept descending until he hit something solid and passed out.

How long he lay there, he did not know, but when he opened his eyes, he could see nothing except a dim blue light. He gave a low moan, as he felt the bruises caused by the long fall.

"You are awake then!" said a tiny voice.

Veleri stirred, and found that he was covered in the ice that he had brought down with him, but he managed to struggle to sit upright and wipe his visor clean. At first, he thought that the voice was from his radio, and then he was aware that something was looking at him.

"Can you speak?" the voice asked. The eyes were a very pale blue, and just discernible against the blue ice.

"Who – who are you?" Veleri croaked.

"Me, I am called Me!" the pale image answered.

"You live down here?" Veleri asked.

"Down, up, what is the difference?"

'*Quite a lot!*' Veleri thought.

"Not really!" the image surprisingly answered his thought.

"You can read my mind?" Veleri was shocked.

"What is 'mind'," the image asked.

"That which creates thoughts,"

"What are 'thoughts'," the image continued asking.

Veleri realised that it was becoming a difficult and complicated discussion, and changed the subject, "Are there others like you?"

"I am me! What are 'others'?"

"I came here with other creatures like me," Veleri attempted an explanation, "that is what 'others' means."

"There are 'others' down here, but not a Me," the image said, *"we are all different."*

A shower of ice fell from above, and Veleri looked up to see the tiny and distant figure belaying down towards him, "That up there is an 'other'."

There was no answer, and when he looked, the image had disappeared as though it had melted into the blue ice. He waited as the figure drew near, it was Tegth.

"You left very suddenly," Tegth smiled, "Was it something I said?" He looked around, "Who were you talking to?"

"I was talking to Me," Veleri smiled as he thought of the confusion.

His rescuer attached the cable to Veleri's suit, and they began the ascent.

"Are you alright?" Resta asked anxiously when they arrived back on the surface. She checked his hands and arms.

"Just bruised and a little confused, thank you" Veleri answered.

"We can continue on our journey then," Jib said.

"Well, no!" Veleri surprised them, "I had a conversation down there with something interesting, either that or I was talking to myself."

"You found something?" Resta said.

"You could say that I stumbled upon it!" Veleri said

with a smile, "Something intelligent and wonderful lives down there, and it may have prevented me from falling further."

"So you do believe that there is life in this wilderness?" Tegth said, with a note of triumph in his voice.

Veleri nodded, "It brings into question what is meant by the term 'life', but there is something down there that needs investigating!"

"Perhaps it is investigating us!" Tegth suggested, only partly in fun.

"Shall we set traps?" Jib asked.

"I don't think that we have the kind of trap needed," Veleri replied, "I am not at all sure if this creature exists as we understand it. It is part of the planet!"

THE TOWN SPIRE

When they came to the New Lands, the decision was made that everything should be new, so it was decided that there should be a New Religion, and a New Church, out with the old and in with the new. Unfortunately, not everyone agreed that it was right and proper to dismiss the old as unwanted. The older folks banged their walking sticks and cried out through their mummified lips that they wanted the familiar and comfortable. Father Chevens stood out firmly to build a church in the old style and called St Botulph's Church, and he had his way with a lot of grumbling from the congregation, or at least from the younger ones.

Boulders were sliced squarely from the mountains and shaped for the building, and in a short time, the yellow sandstone building rose gleaming in the sunlight in the middle of New Town. The prayer-books were printed in the New Religion, not with black covers but in gleaming gold; on this, the congregation won the argument.

Chevens did win the right to decorate the church with gargoyles and grotesques; he said, "It was fitting to remember that evil exists everywhere". The remaining discussion was whether the church tower should have a spire; even Chevens was not certain of this, so for the time being it was finished with a square

Norman tower with four clock faces.

The stonemasons were cleverly inventing all sorts of demonic shapes for the gargoyles, and they were reminded that in ancient times, it was common for the caricatures of prominent people to be displayed on the buildings: the mayor, the chief constable, and naturally, Father Chevens were the first to be mounted on the walls amongst the winged and wingless oddities.

The first service was conducted with full pomp and ceremony. The Archbishop was invited to consecrate the New Church, and he stood admiring the construction and the hideous gargoyles and grotesques for some time relating to stories of great churches. In their colourful robes and carrying a great golden cross, they entered the church with the bells ringing out joyfully to announce the coming of the Saviour to the town, and then came out hurriedly and unceremoniously: the church was full of a sickening stench!

The stonemasons donned the pressure suits used in space and scoured the building; they tapped on the stones and listened intently, they x-rayed the walls and the floors and poked around in the high wooden ceiling, but they could not find the source of the smell. The accusation was that they had buried some dead creature within the golden walls.

Over the next few months, the smell diminished to the faintest of odours with the assistance of paper caches of herbs and bouquets of sweet smelling flowers, and it could be tolerated by the public. Father Chevens settled in and delivered some well-appreciated sermons, and every Sunday the congregation increased.

Everything appeared to go well, that is until the first baptisement, and then all hell let loose! The baptismal font had an intricately carved wooden cover, depicting the same or similar images along the walls, and when the heavy cover was removed, it was found that the holy water had turned green and was covered with an obnoxious slime. There was an uproar that someone had vandalised the church, and then they remembered the horrid smell of the first service and connected the two incidents: someone was playing sick games with the population and Father Chevens initiated strong prayers for the guilty person.

It was some months later, after the font was cleaned, polished and refilled, that someone started counting the gargoyles and grotesques and they called Father Chevens out to confirm the total number.

He stared up at the roof-line and ticked off on his fingers, "I remember that I ordered a gargoyle for each corner and halfway along the nave, and the grotesques as intermediaries," he said, "and the interior should duplicate in wood the external decorations."

The sometime mathematician thrust the paper under the Father's nose, "There is exactly twice that number!" Sure enough, Chevens saw that each stone figure had another by its side as though it had given a stone birth to a twin. The internal wooden figures had also duplicated themselves.

"I will have to check with the builders, but I am sure that I only paid for the number I agreed on!" Father Chevens checked his accounts, and everyone saw that he was correct. For some reason, the stonemason's records had disappeared that added to everyone's suspicions.

"Well Father," insisted the stonemason, "You have a surprise bargain, but we never made those figures!"

"We have an unknown benefactor!" Father Chevens concluded, but he could not have been further from the truth.

As the year passed on, there was no more vandalisation, and those matters were relegated to an ugly history. Early one morning, Father Chevens and the sexton were walking along the nave in deep conversation, when they heard a noise above their heads; it sounded like a pigeon with that distinctive clapping of its wings. They looked at the high ceiling but could see nothing.

"I'll get up there and see if it is making a nest," the sexton promised.

The following day, the sexton borrowed a very long ladder from the fire department who came along to help. The ladder was lodged just under one of the inner double grotesques, and the sexton climbed up, stopping occasionally to look around the roof to see if anything unusual was lodging there.

Finally, he reached the top and placed a hand on the grotesque's snarling head which brought him face to face with its twin – and it winked at him! Then it stuck out its tongue! Surprised and terrified, the sexton slid down the ladder to the floor, hitting his chin on the rungs several times, and ran out of the door. He was found an hour later, very inebriated in the local bar.

Since nobody else had seen what the grotesque had done, it remained a mystery for a while, as the sexton refused to say what had happened. Father Chevens shrugged his shoulders and carried on after finding a new sexton, but every morning he heard the clapping of wings and looked up to see nothing untoward.

As the end of September arrived, the noise of clapping wings became commonplace, and rather than repeat the old sexton's 'accident', Chevens said over the display of potatoes, giant onions, larger pumpkins, and apples for the Harvest Festival, that all birds were God's creatures and were welcome in His House. That was a big mistake! You should never invite the devil into your house!

The carpenters had carved on the wood panels throughout the church, adding decorations everywhere, including the demonic figures and miniature angels. These were included in Chevens' study, the grotesques standing proud of the panelling while the angels stood demurely in small alcoves.

One Friday morning, while writing for the following Sunday service, Chevens leaned back in his chair for inspiration and realised that the top of the study walls was crammed with wooden figures. They appeared to be hugging each other, far more than had been ordered or that he remembered being there before and there was not a space between them. The Father stood up quickly and backed out of the room. After thinking about it and calming down, he peeked round the door and saw that they were still there.

He took a glass of sacramental wine and thought about what he should do. He decided to close the church on the pretext that they would finally add the spire; at least that would give him time to sort out the mess. Despite being a clergyman, Chevens did not believe that these that there was anything devilish about the carvings.

October the thirty-first changed his mind! This is the

Halloween Festival, All Saint's Eve, or the pagan Samhain, the end of summer. The churchyard was still young and did not contain many graves, but candles were lit and placed on the graves as custom dictates.

As dusk fell, the shadows growing longer and more mysterious, great orange pumpkins carved in devilish forms were lit, imitating the grotesques, and children in costumes and masks, also imitating the grotesques, poured on to the streets, a tumult of young laughing voices knocking on doors and crying, "Trick or Treat?"

New Town was exactly that, a new town, and there were perhaps twelve-hundred children of school age. The number of children on the streets on that Samhain night was closer to two-and-one-half thousand, and the costumes were very realistic on most. Even more realistic was that households that did not produce the treats, or ones that the 'children' had not appreciated, had strange experiences.

As bedtime for little ones approached, Father Chevens was standing in the church entrance talking to the police chief. They were in a jovial mood until the police radio beeped and informed them of some strange incidents. At the same moment, Chevens looked up and saw that all of the gargoyles and grotesques had disappeared!

His mouth agape, his finger pointing at the naked roof, Chevens could only stutter. The police chief looked up but did not realise what the problem was, and with apologies, he raced off to the nearest incident, the siren wailing and adding to the growing mayhem.

The hospital had also been summoned to the incidents that turned out to be intractable. People were talking in unknown tongues, and some had broken out in green spots, others had grown old with white hair, and others had assumed their youthful appearance. The most frightening was the appearance of old and deceased members of the family wandering down streets that were named after them; later they found that the graves and coffins had been opened and the urns removed from their niches.

In the first light of dawn, everything reverted to normal. The dead were back in their graves, although the headstones were a little askew. The ashes were back in the urns, but there was some uncertainty as to which ashes returned to which urns. Spots had disappeared, people were talking intelligible words, and they all looked the correct age. Only the gargoyles and grotesques had not returned to their places in St Botulph's Church.

Although that was a worry, Father Chevens was temporarily relieved. The spire grew and clad in copper that quickly turned bright green. St Lucia was celebrated with white-robed girls carrying bright candles. Christmas came without incident, except that a few of the congregation became embarrassingly drunk, and New Year was brought in with a speech and the ringing of the church bells and the eruption of fireworks, screaming rockets bursting with colourful fiery blooms high over the town. Father Chevens and most of his flock began to relax and forget the past.

A dreadful storm started in the last week of March, the heavens darkened, the swollen and swirling clouds taking on fantastic shapes and malignant colours, and rain and hail erupted from them. The last day of March is Walpurgis Eve, and Walpurgisnacht is when Shatain calls to the demons. It is also called the Night of the Witches.

Normally, there would be a service in the Church with a choir, but the weather was so dreadful that it was cancelled. Walpurgisnacht was also the night that the gargoyles and grotesques returned, this time with the great sound of flapping wings as from a large aviary, with cries and screams that could be heard all over the town.

Chevens rushed to the church and swung open the heavy oak doors. Standing in front of the golden cross was a tall glaring figure in red; massive black horns sprang from its head, and fangs dripped from the gaping wolf snout. Its feet were cloven hooves, and a barbed tail lashed furiously back and forth. Raising its claws upwards, it began to chant loudly in an unknown language, occasionally laughing demonically.

Hazy figures started to appear from aether floating everywhere, and the gargoyles and grotesques were racing round and round, screaming and roaring obscenities. It was a circus of the damned!

Father Chevens sank to his knees and began to pray as he had never prayed before, the rosary beads passing rapidly through his slippery fingers. The night was split by lightning, and the thunder hardly covered the calling of Shatain to his demons; it was as though the storm was competing with the evil presence. Chevens prayed harder, the sweat pouring down his face.

And then a miracle! A bolt of lightning struck the spire, the blue flash reaching down to the golden cross and arching over to the ranting red figure. The air was full of the choking smell of ozone and incense. With a heart-stopping scream, the crimson figure vanished in a black cloud, as did the demons that were forming from the aether, and the gargoyles and grotesques burst into motes of dust.

Small pieces of wood and sandstone were cleared up on for a week, none of them recognisable as any creature. The spire was damaged, bent and crooked like a witch's hat; Chevens refused to mend it, instead, reinforcing it to stand that way for eternity. The golden cross was partially melted, but that was also left as a memorial.

The many gargoyles and grotesques had vanished completely never to return, and it was assumed that they were the cause behind the weird incidents. During the following service, Father Chevens said, "We had brought the evil with us, in our hearts and minds; fortunately, we also brought the good spirits."

Now, whenever Chevens hears the flutter of wings, he starts and then smiles, and when the storm rages and thunders, he raises his hat and gives thanks to the good lightning.

THE FOUNDLING

The doctor's surgery was placed centrally in the town so that it was in more or less equal distance for everyone. That was where the crib was laid, on the step on a cold winter's night with snowflakes dancing through the light beams.

The receptionist was going home when she almost stepped on the small package. It was wrapped up against the weather in an old blanket, but it would not have survived the night, and there were rumours of foxes or worse in the area at night, patrolling the streets and gardens.

Doctor Radlom Bercy thoroughly checked the gurgling infant, a boy, and the child was in perfect health and about a month old. He checked his records but could find no trace of a mother that would fit the bill, not in his district at least.

"Well young man, what are we to call you?" The dark eyes looked back into his, and for a moment, it was as though the child understood: a window had opened between them and thoughts and emotions passed between them. Thoughtfully, he returned the baby to the crib and pondered on the experience.

The receptionist Glaia volunteered to look after the baby for the night; there were empty beds, and she could place the crib next to one of them. The doctor checked on them before going home, and both were sleeping with identical little sighs.

"I gave Tithy his breakfast this morning; he loves oats," Glaia informed him in the morning; she appeared radiant and happy.

"That is his name is it, Tithy?" Radlom smiled, "Where did you find that?"

The answer made the doctor stop in mid-stride, "He told me it was his name!"

He turned and looked at the baby and Gaia, "He spoke to you?"

Gaia frowned, "No, not really; it was as though the thought appeared in my head. I woke up this morning, and I understood him."

The doctor approached the crib and was surprised to see that the toddler was standing on two feet and hanging on to the wooden bars, "So your name is Tithy!"

'Yes' came the thought, *'and your name is Radlom'*.

Radlom sat down with a thump, "This little fellow is telepathic!" he stared back at the infant through the bars of the crib.

"That is what I thought, but that is silly, isn't it?" Gaia said, "Tithy says that it is normal, being telepathic I mean!"

Radlom looked towards the crib and saw the dark eyes looking at him, *'You are not to worry,'* came the thought, *'I can look after all of us.'*

"I'm sure that you can!" grunted the doctor, "Can you read our minds, every little thought?"

'If I want to, but I sense that you are uncomfortable with that idea.'

"We like our privacy," Radlom replied, "There are some things deep within us that would be embarrassing if everyone knew."

'Likewise, I would not reveal everything I sense, as that would hurt many people.'

"Thank you for small mercies," Radlom rubbed his chin, "When I first saw you last night, I guessed that you were only a couple of weeks old, but now you are standing."

'You are correct! I am just over two weeks old, but I develop quickly; I even have all of my teeth!' To prove that, Tithy gave a brilliant baby smile, and then burped.

"I think that he needs some relief from the wind," Gaia had been looking at the pair of them and listening to the one-sided conversation, "He is telepathic, isn't he?"

"Oh yeah, and I think with knobs on!" Radlom was thinking hard, "For now, we keep this between ourselves, and that goes for you young man especially!"

'No problem!' came the thought.

A week later and Radlom was addressing a serious-faced five-year-old, "Can you hear everyone's thought all at the same time?"

Tithy shook his head, and as he spoke in his childlike voice via his mouth, Radlom could also hear the serious adult voice in his head.

"I can read everyone in the universe, I have that ability, but that way leads to madness: I have to apply filters and also focus so that only you can hear my thoughts. If you were in a crowded room, can you understand when everyone is talking? No, you concentrate; focus on those nearest to you."

Radlom nodded, "I can understand that! You say that you can read everyone in the universe, how many minds are there?"

Tithy smiled, and the voice in the doctor's head laughed, *"I am sure that there must be a name for such a large number, but it is almost countless. Some of the thoughts I do not understand as they concern things unknown to me, and I should imagine that you would not understand as well."*

"From the very first time that I met you, your language was well developed," Radlom said, "Was all of the words in your head from your birth?"

A little frown creased the child's face, *"Yes and no! I heard your minds as soon as I was conscious, and the meanings come with the words."*

"It sounds as though the meanings are more like emotions," Radlom said, "perhaps the words are also emotions, or linked to that part of the brain that deals with emotions."

"I could ask someone out there," Tithy's finger pointed upwards.

"You mean an alien?" Radlom was surprised, but then realised that there were no limits to the child's mind.

"I have to be careful," Tithy said, *"Those with the best knowledge on the subject are also telepaths and could sense my questions."*

"Why is that dangerous?" Radlom asked.

"My brain is still in its infancy, and some of those others have minds that could tear mine apart!" Tithy looked into Radlom's face, and the doctor could hear the fear in his mind.

"If there is any danger, it can wait!" Radlom patted the boy's dark curls.

Radlom placed the boy far away from the town with an old man who preferred to live a lonely life in the mountains. This was necessary, as Tithy's physical development would have attracted unwanted attention. The old mountain man listened and nodded, as he understood what loneliness was, and that people that were different were often unwanted. They still kept in touch telepathically, and Radlom was amazed at the remarkable development that the young man had achieved. A young adult man of six months of age had an impressive strength of mind!

Tithy developed the ability to take Radlom's mind into his, and the pair of them hurtled through space to visit other worlds, and he rode piggy-back into people's minds. It helped him to achieve remarkable results in the medical world, since the patient's mind knew more than the patient did. He also upset people at council meetings by 'seeing' what really was the other's selfish intentions.

After five years, Radlom paid a visit to the mountains and was shocked at Tithy's appearance: he was no longer a child or a young man; he was a wizened old man with a wrinkled face and hands, stooped and with a whisper of a voice.

'It is good that you came,' the old man said/thought, *'in a short while I will terminate, and this will be the last conversation we shall have.'*

Radlom protested, but Tithy laid a liver spotted-hand on his arm, *"There is no need for sorrow, in this short life I have experienced more than anyone you know."*

"But you have much more to give!" Radlom said, covering the old hand with his own, "I have never asked you, but where did you come from?"

Silently, Tithy pointed down at the soft earth, *"I came from here,"* he placed a finger on Radlom's forehead, *"and from there! I am a product of your mind!"*

Radlom's mouth opened in surprise, but Tithy closed his eyes, and the wrinkled, spotted hand went cold.

ROAD STOP

Mio Prapas drove down the new road between the high Blue Mountains; the tyres hummed on the smooth black surface, squealing on the bends as he kept the shiny new sports car at high speed. The mountain tops began to glow as the first sun rose, and soon the second smaller globe will follow its larger sibling.

The cool passing wind ruffled his tawny hair, fluttering it around his ears. The radio was softly playing some old song, a very old song called 'It's a Wonderful World', and Mio thought that it certainly was! The forest of trees gave the area a special perfume, subtle and satisfying.

The road through the mountains had been opened a week ago; they had bored through the tough rock and scooped out pebbles and sand, enough to make a new hill. That was what Mio loved about this planet, everything was new, but he was surprised that someone had quickly claimed the land by the road beside the Crystal Clear Lake so soon. On that patch of land, someone had erected an eating house, a structure painted in bright colours, and neon lights proclaiming 'Syti's Fine Foods' to attract the passing traffic.

Mio was the only passing traffic, so he obligingly

pulled in. On opening the glass door, he was greeted by a draft of air-conditioning and the warm scent of fresh coffee. Behind the bar lined with blue seated stools, was an attractive blonde woman laying out a variety of cakes.

"What can I get you, Honey?" she asked with a bright smile.

Mio smiled back, "I'll start with some coffee, thanks. How long have you been open?"

"Oh, my grandpa has owned this land for a while, and when they put the road out there, it seemed natural to open the road stop." She poured out the coffee.

"It seems pretty quiet!" Mio pulled the coffee towards him.

"It will pick up once people realise we are here," She pushed a menu towards him, "Early days yet, but grandpap says that soon we will be complaining of overwork!"

Mio nodded, "I'll have some ham and eggs thanks!"

"We have our own pigs and chickens," She went into the kitchen, "so no middlemen!"

"And guaranteed fresh!" Mio called out.

While he waited for the food, he turned on his stool and looked out of the windows, "Sure is a pretty spot: you are lucky! Is there any fish in the lake?"

"Stocked it myself with rainbow trout!" The voice was not that of the blonde woman; it was gruff and old. Mio spun back and came face to face with an old man with a few whiskers on his chin. "Pris made this breakfast for you, and we have some fresh buttered bread."

"I was just admiring the scenery," Mio picked up the knife and fork, breathing in the mouth-watering aroma of the ham.

"I heard you," the old man said, "My grandfather had it given to him by a friend that owed him. We were wondering what to do with it when we heard that the road was passing by."

"That was lucky!" Mio said through a mouthful of food.

"Not really!" the old man leaned forward on his elbows, "This is the only valley through the mountains for miles, so it was obvious that a road would appear sometime."

Mio paused in eating his breakfast and turned back to the scenery as he drank some coffee, "I wouldn't mind living here, it is idyllic!"

"We would like you to stay with us for a while," a new voice said. When Mio turned back, there were three people staring back at him, the blonde Pris, Grandpapa, and a young man, a younger version of Grandpapa. "We are thinking to start some settlement here."

"I haven't heard about a new town out here," Mio said. There was something odd about the way all three were looking at him.

"We don't need permission out here," Grandpapa growled, "We own this land and the rights to do as we want with it!"

"Who said that you could do that?" Mio asked.

"The Emperor of All You See!" They spoke in unison, "He would like to meet you."

Mio shook his head; the three figures were becoming blurred, and they were moving around the floor without walking, they were floating, and Mio realised that they had no legs to walk on. He stood to leave, but they were blocking his escape. He made it to the door, staggering like a drunk, and when he opened it, a tall figure in scarlet robes beckoned him to step forward.

Behind the robed figure, Mio could see sail-boats on the Crystal Clear Lake, and on the shore there were shining white buildings, some short and wide, others wider and taller.

"What is this?" Mio cried out.

"We have lived here for aeons, beyond time recalling," The robed figure said in a sombre voice, "We are the True People of this planet. You may join us if that is your real wish."

Mio turned to look back at the road stop, but it was another shining white building, and instead of three members of a family in the doorway, there was just one, robed as the other. As he looked it changed from the young man, and then the old man and then the woman Pris, and they cycled through the images.

He had begun to feel uneasy from the moment that he ordered the meal; there was something strange about the setup, now he felt panic. "What if I choose not to?" Mio asked.

The air was cool in the valley, a brook ran alongside the road, sparkling and gurgling over rocks and pebbles, the scent of the pine trees was like a vague perfume. The engine purred, and the tyres sang a song of the road.

"Yes!" shouted Mio, "It is a wonderful world!"

THE CARETAKER

Infinity Apartments had been built in a rush during the initial landing; designed to be a temporary accommodation during the frantic period of the planning of the New Town; it was hastily built of clapboard and shingles, nailed together in a flurry of hammer blows. Inevitably, it had stayed in use and become dilapidated and an uncomfortable home to cockroaches and mice, as well as the oldest inhabitants, people who remembered the old times, and told stories of deep space and multi-coloured stars beyond measure while they sipped mundane warm beverages through tinder-dry lips.

The Caretaker was only slightly younger than the residents were; he would listen at half-open doors while he leaned on a broom to the stories that were whispered like secrets across a dusty room, the mice would stay silent as they also listened in dark corners and the cockroaches ceased to scurry behind the yellowing walls.

The old folk spoke of blazing stars so gigantic that it took weeks to pass them, giant red stars that were in the last stages of their short lives. The ship had travelled through immense dust clouds that were illuminated by intense bright blue stars, child stars that were beginning their lives in the dusty nurseries. Ancient stars that had begun to shine before time had begun, long before the other stars were born; now brown burned out husks with just the faint flicker of light from deep within the charred remnants. There were small stars that were gravitational giants, attracting new material to burn, consuming other stars and planets, streamers of gas and dust leading into the fiery maw.

At night, the Caretaker would stand outside and look above the Blue Mountains to see the stars; which one did they come from? When he asked the old folk that question, they would be confusing, telling different stories; some said that it was a burning desert, others that it was a frozen globe, and others that it was an endless sea full of strange creatures. He knew that none of them had seen the home planet, like him, they were all born on the long voyage, so these were guesses on their part born of ancient tales.

Somewhere in the firmament, was the ship that they had arrived on, silently drifting around the New Planet, the New Home. They unloaded everything to bring down to the surface; the landing craft fell like hailstones bringing machines for making other machines. Most of them walked, crawled or rolled by themselves, lights blinking and producing peculiar noises as though they were talking and grumbling to themselves, while others were escorted by mechanical attendees.

The Caretaker remembered that: as a small child, he had watched the parade of machines making for destinations into the deep dark forests, into the Blue Mountains, under the seas, and others starting to dig the foundations of New Town. Snaking around the digging machines and off to distant places, new roads were lain, black and sinuous.

New Town Library was part of New Town Museum, an annexe to the History of The Voyage. The Caretaker visited the library, intent on finding the answers that vexed him. There were mountains of information, books and pictures, documentaries and examples of clothing, but very little on the Planet of Origin. It was as though they wanted to forget.

In one book were some pictures of naked, hairy bipeds that were labelled as their far distant relatives. They had protruding snouts and fangs like some wild predator; the Caretaker felt his chin and ran his tongue over his teeth, wondering how they could be his relatives. Other books were written in a strange language that was impossible to understand, and that added to his confusion and frustration.

There were many books that presented unusual people who could fly, some with wings and some without. Others had strange powers, such as turning people into animals and vice-versa, and terrifying monsters of tremendous size. There was one book he found about a girl lost in a make-believe land, and other books where there were witches and wizards, and evil powers that had to be defeated. The Caretaker thought that they were as fanciful as the hairy relatives were.

Even more confusing and more than a little frightening were the stories of Gods, strange omnipotent beings who created storms, floods, and devastated towns. They were escorted by winged beasts, the Dragons, and vicious little demons that torment the soul.

The Caretaker had not experienced a storm until landing on New Home, and he was terrified by the sound, the power, the lightning, and thunder. It was explained to him afterwards, but he could not accept that, the Gods were much more logical to him. Every storm would send him scurrying to hide in the dark with the mice and cockroaches.

He was in awe of the old people, who cast a single glance at the raging weather through the window and carried on whispering their stories, sucking on straws of lemonade. Did they possess strange powers that nullified the Gods, witches, and wizard's powers?

During his reading, he came across a mention several times of an altar, something that served to placate the Gods. He built a small shrine in the quiet garden of Infinity Apartments. He had no idea of what a shrine should look like, but he placed a few personal items on some flat stones, and once a day, at dawn before the others had awakened, he knelt before the shrine and asked for protection.

The storms kept coming despite the prayers, and eventually, a bolt of lightning struck the simple shrine and destroyed it. The Caretaker was in terror! He expected that at any time, one of the Gods to arrive and take his soul.

He made his way to St Botulph's Church to seek guidance and protection there. Father Chevens listened to the Caretaker's story with patience and understanding. He explained about the reason for religion, that there was a single deity that created everything, and that thunder and lightning were part of that creation. The storms brought rain that was important to the cycle of life, and it should be respected and not feared. The God had many names.

Here was something that the Caretaker could understand, and so every Sunday he would arrive at the church doors and was the first to enter. Chevens realised that it was easier for the Caretaker to understand the idea of a single God than to work through the confusion of scientific theories.

The Caretaker now listened openly to the whispers

of the old people; he understood that they had witnessed the results of the Creation during their journey. He sat outside the ring of old people, just listening without saying a word. It amused the old folk, and some of the stories were exaggerations for their own amusement and to tease the Caretaker.

The Gods produced miracles, impossible, illogical things, and if that were true, then there could be wizards and dragons that could also perform miracles. He sat patiently with the old folk, listening to their tales and waiting for the miracles to happen.

The storms came and he no longer flinched, confident that they did not destroy, only create. He saw a tree burst into flame after being struck by lightning, and viewed the stump as something that a God had created.

The Caretaker no longer moved the brush or mop, he sat and listened and soon began to dream. The dust settled on everything, the mice peered at the group from dark and dusty corners, and the cockroaches continued to scurry behind the walls.

SHANTY TOWN

One of the long black sinuous roads led to Shanty Town, perched on the shore of the largest ocean on the planet. Wim followed the road as it tracked beside the Fresh River to the town; he walked the whole distance, occasionally accepting a lift from a passing truck.

As he topped the rise before the town, he saw for the first time the expanse of blue water that stretched endlessly over the horizon. He could hardly believe his eyes that so much water could exist! Eagerly, he ran down the road and into town, passing shops selling everything from fresh vegetables, to fresh bread and fine costumes. He arrived breathlessly at the quayside, bent down and ran his fingers through the ripples of water; it was real!

Smiling, almost laughing, he turned and saw a stall full of the products of the ocean; there were fish of all sizes, all colours and hues, and crab and lobster, and eels still moving. On one side were shrimp of all sizes, some as big as his hand, and some strange creatures he could not identify.

"New in town, are you?" a voice by his side made him jump.

He nodded speechlessly at the fishmonger's question.

The fishmonger was round and cheerful; wiping his hands on his striped apron, he held out a damp hand, "Everyone reacts in the same way when they see the ocean for the very first time! It is huge, almost incomprehensibly huge and full of mystery."

"Mystery?" Wim looked surprised and eager.

"That is my boat," He pointed to a fishing vessel on the quayside, "My son Con captains it now, and he has brought more than fish to our table. Here he comes now; ask him about what he finds in the ocean."

A young man wearing a peaked cap approached them; the similarity to the fishmonger was apparent.

"This here young fellow is new to town and would like to hear some of your stories," the fishmonger said.

The young man laughed, "Every newcomer arrives outside Dad's shop, attracted to the sights, sounds and smells of the sea." For the first time, Wim noticed the smell of the ozone. "Come into the shop and take a drink while I'll tell you what I know."

They drank hot sweet tea as they sat at the table, and as Con spoke, they helped themselves to fresh pink shrimps.

"First of all, no one knows very much about the ocean," Con began, "As you can see it is immense, but it is also deep, and down there where light does not shine are some extraordinary creatures." He spoke of grey whales that were larger than his ship, of fast-moving shoals of small fish and the creatures that hunt them. But deeper down were the very strange animals of all, some with eight arms, several eyes on the ends of stalks, fish with mouths so enormous that they could eat twice their weight in a single gulp. There were other things down there that he hinted at that were more terrible than anyone could imagine. "It is a savage place!" he concluded.

"I would love to see it!" Wim said.

"Tomorrow, I am going out for a week or so," Con said, "if you want you can come along, but I warn you that it is not safe or comfortable."

The fishmonger provided a bed for the night, and at the break of day, Wim stepped on board a ship for the first time in his life. The first thing that he noticed was that the ship constantly moved; it was like a live animal, impatient to sail into the unknown.

He watched what the three men were doing under Con's instruction, while holding on to a rail as he tried to keep his balance on the heaving deck. That also produced the problem of sea-sickness, and he spent some time leaning over the side.

When he recovered, the ship was trailing a net, and after an hour or so, the net was winched on board. Wim joined the others in sorting out the fish, and he expressed amazement at the huge variety.

"Throw back the very small fish," Con instructed, "and watch your fingers, some of them have sharp teeth!"

Night fell, and they still worked on the catch, Wim learning quickly about the variety of fish. When they had finished, Wim crawled tiredly into a bunk and fell asleep; he was not disturbed by the rolling of the ship or the thump of the engines.

The week passed quickly, and Wim developed a ruddy tan from the wind, sun and salt water. When they berthed at the quayside, Wim leapt onto the shore and found that he had trouble walking; it felt as though the ground was moving! He was advised that the sensation would soon pass.

On the first morning after returning, Wim went for a walk along the shore. He had learned more in the week than he had during the rest of his life; he had a new perspective to appreciate and think about. He sat on a rock and was surprised that he had walked so far; Shanty Town was out of sight.

The water just below his feet was very clear; he could see the sand and pebbles and even a small crab moving sideways as they do.

A little way out where the water was deeper, he saw some fish swimming near the surface, and occasionally a wide silvered tail would flash into the sunlight. He thought back to the trip and tried to place them among those they had caught.

Suddenly, one of the fish swam quickly towards him, and it came to rest below him, and it looked up. It had a human face! Green hair floated down to its waist, and two arms were held up towards him. The top of the creature was naked, and the breasts indicated that it was female, but from the waist down it was all fish.

Wim stared back and felt an urge to reach down and seize the arms held out to him. The face was that of an angel, beautiful and smiling, and the attraction was obvious. Music could be heard, a choir and he realised that the creature and its friends were singing. He felt himself sliding into the sea and into the welcoming arms.

At the end of the day, the fishmonger was surprised that Wim had not returned. Con was wondering what had become of the new ship-hand, "Perhaps he found something else to interest him," he said.

"Or perhaps he found one of those mermaids you are always on about!" the fishmonger laughed.

Con didn't laugh, instead he looked longingly out past the harbour and across the ocean.

THE GIFT

"*He* is very clever Mum!" Jenn said.

Mother pummelled the dough, spreading flour over the kitchen and her children, "Who is clever, sweetheart?"

"Our new friend," Keth, Jenn's twin brother answered, wiping the flour from his eyes.

"What makes him clever?" Mother turned the dough.

"He can do all sorts of things," Jenn answered.

Mother paused, "Who is this friend? What is his name and how old is he?"

The twins looked at each other, "I guess he is about our age," Keth said uncertainly.

"He has a great name!" Jenn said positively, "It is Hura."

"Where did you meet him?"

"You know that pond where we caught that strange fish?" Jenn said, "It was on the path that leads there."

"Who caught the fish?" Keth demanded. Jenn

ignored him.

Mother turned back to the dough, "Bring him home sometime."

The twins raced up the stairs to their rooms. "You didn't tell Mum what he gave us!" Jenn said.

"He said it was a secret!" Keth reminded her.

"It is not right to keep secrets from Mum!" Jenn frowned.

"But he said that it was a real secret!" Keth held a finger up to his lips.

"Where is it?"

Keth brought out the secret from beneath his overall. It glowed with a pulsating energy in the palm of his hand; at first glance, it appeared like a bird's egg, and then its outline changed to a crystal ball with a small furnace of blue in the centre.

Jenn's voice dropped to an almost inaudible whisper, "What did he say it did?"

"Anything that we wanted it to," Keth's voice imitated his sister's whisper.

Jenn sat back and frowned at the device, "It looks as though it is alive! I think that we should give it back to Hura!"

"It is rude to give presents pack!" Keth objected.

"What does it mean, 'anything we want'?" Jenn wriggled further away from the device which had started to whisper all to itself, "What if we want something bad?"

"Come on, Sis," Keth closed his hand over the whisper, "I don't think that it is anything bad."

"Perhaps not, but what about us?" Jenn stood up, "people can be bad!"

Keth turned his back on his sister and mumbled, "I am keeping it!"

On the following morning, Jenn was bright and breezy, "Let us go and find Hura," she suggested eagerly.

"He is not there!" Keth said sourly.

"How do you know?" Jenn said, "Come on!"

"OK, I'll come with you, just to prove that I'm right!" Keth said.

Almost angrily, he led the way down to the pond, and Hura was nowhere to be seen, "There, I told you!"

"If we wait around, he will turn up," Jenn said with conviction.

"I told you, he has gone away!" Keth turned back to the path.

"How do you know that?" Jenn demanded, "He never said anything while we were with him!"

Keth shrugged and kept walking back home. Jenn crossed her arms and sat down angrily, determined to meet their new friend. After the considerable long time of ten minutes, she followed her brother.

Over the next few days, Keth became very secretive, preferring to stay alone. He also became sullen and almost violent towards Jenn.

Mother noticed, "Have you and Keth had an argument?"

Jenn shook her head so violently that she felt sick, and then she burst out, "He has been that way since we met Hura!"

"That new friend?"

Jenn nodded, but not as rapidly as before, "Not really a friend, we only met him the once, and Keth says that he has gone away, but Hura never said that! I have been to the pond every day, but he has not appeared."

"Perhaps he said something, and you didn't hear," Mother said.

"I am not deaf!" Jenn said angrily.

It was the following day that Jenn met someone at the pond; it was not Hura, but a girl that looked like him, "Hello, I am Nitha. Are you waiting for Hura?"

Jenn nodded dumbly.

"He has gone away for a time, but he will be back," The girl cocked her head, "I thought that he said there were two of you."

"Yeah, my brother Keth," Jenn sat down of a fallen tree.

"Has he gone moody?" Nitha asked. Jenn nodded and started crying.

"Did Hura give him anything?" Nitha asked, and Jenn nodded, "We would like that back as it was not his to give away," Nitha continued.

"What is it?" Jenn asked through her tears.

"It is different things to different people, but it has altered your brother," Nitha said, "Can you get it or him down here?"

After a pause, Jenn nodded, "If you wait here, I will fetch him."

She found Keth hiding in the tool-shed, "I have

found someone who knows Hura and would like to meet you. Can you come to the pond now?"

Keth hesitated and then stuffing something in his pocket, he nodded and followed Jenn. She had a good idea that he had stuffed the object into his pocket, but she thought that there would be a problem to make him hand it back.

Nitha stood and smiled as they came down the path, "Hello, I am Hura's sister Nitha, and you must be Keth!"

Keth hesitated, and then with a nervous smile came and sat down on the fallen tree. Nitha came and sat next to him while Jenn stood and watched nervously.

"Hura is very sorry that he had to go away, but he will return in due course. He liked both of you, and I can see why," Nitha took hold of Keth's hands, "I would like to be your friend as well!"

Keth stammered and tried to remove his hands, but Nitha held them tightly, "I – I would like to be friends t -too. There is just the two of us, and it's exciting to meet someone n - new."

As he spoke, Jenn saw a change come over him; gone was the secretive and angry boy, and it was replaced by a shy and open individual.

"Hura gave you something," said Nitha, "have you

brought it with you?"

Keth nodded and produced it from his pocket. Jenn noticed that Nitha kept a firm hold on his other hand. It was as though she needed to touch him to make him do as she wanted.

With a sigh, she took the object and wrapped it in a bright blue cloth that she took from her overall, "He should not have given it to you as it was not his to give, and it would have done you great harm. I am sorry, but at times Hura can be very mischievous."

Keth almost tried to snatch it back, but Nitha had kept contact with him, and somehow that was enough to control him. Jenn stepped forward, and with a smile, Nitha transferred her grip on Keth's hands to her.

"He will be alright now," Nitha said, "Take him home and let him rest for a day or two."

He was led like a sheep up the path, and when Jenn looked back, she could have sworn that there was more than one person there by the pond, and none of them looked like Hura, Nitha, or the twins, in fact, not like anything she had seen before.

Jenn told Mother that Keth had felt a little sick and she would look after him. Quietly he was led up the stairs and laid on the bed. He never said a word, just closed his eyes and fell into a deep sleep, mother came to the bed and became anxious, but Jenn managed to convince her that all he needed was to rest.

The following morning, he was more talkative, so Jenn asked him a question, "What did you see?"

Keth turned and looked quietly into her eyes, "Everything! I saw us, I saw them, I saw the past and the future. It is becoming faint now and confused, but I saw all of Time!"

Jenn was sitting on the bed next to him when he started to cry. She put her young arms around him, and he clung to her as never before, "Oh Jenn! It was awful! I saw what would happen to us, but there were many variations; sometimes there were good things, but mostly it was terrible!"

"Did you see Nitha at the Pool?" Jenn asked.

Keth stopped crying, at least it was reduced to a snuffle, "She was one of them, the creatures that live here, and so was Hura. When we first met him, I thought that he looked different, and then it was alright!"

"I don't think that they mean us any harm," Jenn rubbed his shoulders, "but I think that we should not accept gifts from strangers."

The following day, Keth was back to normal. Both

Mother and Jenn sighed with relief, but for different reasons. He never mentioned what he had learned, but he became more attentive to Mother and Jenn, almost protective. The strange inhabitants were never seen again.

AUNT MIDDY

It became hot that summer; the greenness of the grass became a different shade of dry, flowers drooped in the direct sun, only to revive in the warm evenings with a proper watering. Gentlemen sought the cool atmosphere in a fine ale; children clamoured for the white mountains of ice-cream and the rivers of soda-pop, ladies of a certain age sat on the front porch and waved fans of warm air over crystal glasses of iced lemonade or mint juleps. It was hot!

Aunt Middy was a formidable member of the latter. Her husband of some thirty years had passed on, and his remains were laid in the dry soil of St Botulph's Churchyard, alongside her unfortunate son, and most of her neighbour's men, except Mr Pold who had lost his charming wife. He helped with the gardens, and in return was provided with cream sponge cakes in the summers and hot stews during the cold winters. He was also a useful hand at canasta and bridge.

Father Chevens would pass by on most days, lifting his hat in greeting and passing a few comments about the weather, but not so often recently; it was cooler within the cold stone confines of the church. Even the hounds and cats found life difficult in the heat, seeking the shade of a bush or under the porches. A few small goldfinches made use of the dust to shake the mites from their brilliant feathers.

The wood of the houses creaked with the heat; the small amount of sap left in the veins became less and creating cracks in the frames and furniture. Mr Pold was kept busy with wood oils to keep the rot at bay; the sweet scent of oil pervaded the area.

A stranger dismounted from the bus that came from New Town; he stood uncertainly in the midday sun with a suitcase in hand. He lifted his hat to shield his eyes and looked around the town square; nothing moved!

He walked with a limp towards the nearest store and entered Jask's Emporium. Jask was asleep behind the cash register with the grey cat that greeted the stranger with a non-committal stare, as cats are wont to do. The stranger coughed twice before Jask woke up.

"Sorry, sorry!" Jask jumped to attention, "It's this damn heat; it just takes the energy out of a soul. What can I do for you, sir?"

"Yes, it is unusually hot," the stranger agreed, "I am looking for an Aunt Middy; she's a relation of mine."

"No problem!" Jask said, "If you turn left out of this door, and go down..." Jask counted on his fingers, "go down twelve houses, and she will probably be sitting on the porch. Can I interest you in a jug of lemonade; it's made locally?" The stranger bought two. As the door closed, Jask and the cat returned to their dreams of frozen winters.

As he passed each house, the stranger greeted the incumbent on the porch by lifting his hat, and his progress was followed by curious eyes as he limped towards Aunt Middy's house. At one house, a small terrier feebly objected to the intrusion and then went back to sleep. He stood at the gate and smiled at Aunt Middy.

"Excuse me dear lady, but I am looking for Aunt Middy."

"You've found her!" Aunt Middy fanned herself furiously, "What can I do for you?"

"I'm your nephew Gorb, from your sister Meln." The stranger continued to smile, but it faltered, as there was no immediate answer.

Eventually, Aunt Middy answered, "What has happened to my stupid sister?"

"She upped and died, but she wanted you to read this letter," Gorb produced a letter, and judging from its condition, it was also suffering from the heat.

"My sister Meln has not written to me in over thirty years, not even a Christmas card, so what does she want me to do now?" Aunt Middy beckoned him to open the gate and approach her presence.

Gorb did so and offered up the damp and wilting letter. Aunt Middy opened the sodden paper with some distaste, placed her rimless glasses on her nose and read the letter; it was an impressive six pages! Occasionally, she harrumphed and sighed, and then read the letter again.

She peered over her rimless glasses at him, "Do you know what is in this letter – Gorb?" she had difficulty in remembering or saying his name.

"Not really," Gorb shook his head, "I do think that it mentions that I need a place to stay."

Aunt Middy nodded, "And she expects me to put up with a lodger! The cheek of it after all of this time! What do you do – Gorb?" The question was fired with all of the energy of a battleship's broadside.

"I sort of help out where needed," He pointed to his left leg, "I had an accident that stopped me from taking a permanent position."

Aunt Middy snorted and removed her rimless glasses, "Come and sit up here while I think!"

They sat together for most of the afternoon, Aunt Middy offered Gorb a lemonade, and he returned the favour with one flask that he bought at Jask's Emporium, but for most of the time, they just sat in silence while Aunt Middy thought through the problem while bees collected the pollen from drooping flower-heads.

Eventually, what she had been waiting for appeared; Mr Pold came round the corner carrying a bucket and followed by his dog. "Mr Pold," Aunt Middy called out, "We have a problem here that you may be able to help us with."

When Pold was standing squarely in front of the formidable lady, she relayed the problem, "You must see that it would not be right or proper for a young man to share this accommodation with me, even if he is a relation." At the last sentence, she sniffed.

"Quite, quite," Pold nodded his head, "Not proper at all!"

"So I thought that as you are now a single gentleman since your dear Pros passed away," Aunt Middy used her most beguiling and honeyed voice, "that you will have room for my nephew, and he would be company for you as well."

Gorb stood up, "I can help with any odd jobs as well!"

Pold was in the horns of a dilemma; he knew that if

he refused Aunt Middy, there would be repercussions, as she would convince the other woman and most of the Town Council, of which she was the chairperson, that they should not avail themselves of his services, and that would be a disaster! On the other hand, he had been accustomed to his own company, keeping his own time-tables and eating, sleeping when he wanted. On the plus side, he could do with a helping hand with the odd jobs.

After a short pause, he brightened up, "I think that it would be an admirable idea, and I could do with an assistant!"

"Well done, Mr Pold," Aunt Middy beamed at him, realising that she had placed him in an awkward position, and an inconvenience, "To settle the deal, with you both come round this evening for a meal? In the meantime, you should show him where he will be staying." Having been dismissed, Gorb thanked his aunt and followed Pold and his dog to his new residence.

The town settled down for the evening, apart from the rumours about the new inhabitant of the Pold household, and the yellow lights appeared in the windows, dimly illuminating the gardens and pathways. The smell of fresh bread filled the avenues, and soon the sound of an old piano or a guitar began to be heard playing old and favourite melodies.

The evenings and nights were hardly any cooler than

in the daytime; moths came and fluttered around the open windows and doors, but prevented from entering due to the mesh doors erected by Pold. An owl hooted near St Botulph's Church, and somewhere far off, a nightingale sang. Lovers strolled hand in hand under a nearly full moon, and the last playing children were called in to brush their teeth and climb into bed.

After the splendid salad provided by Aunt Middy, the three people and the dog sat on the porch, the men drinking beer and Aunt Middy a small concoction of her own. It was pleasant, even if the heat continued. Aunt Middy was satisfied with her arrangement, especially when both Pold and Gorb pronounced that it suited them as well. All was good with the world.

THE MANSION

The great house was built at great expense and even greater effort; the site was chosen to overlook New Town over the New River. That required building the New Road over the New Bridge and up to the doors of the Grand Mansion.

To enable secure foundations, the top of the hill was removed for a level base floor and deep pylons were driven down to the ground rock; the preparation took two years, including the bridge and road. Apart from the trucks driving back and forth, people lost interest in the Grand Mansion, but after the preparation, the building rose very quickly and there were comments and even gasps.

Lok Pren had commissioned the building based on a picture he found in the records; he knew nothing else about it, and employed engineers and architects to sort out the details. It had ten floors and every floor had its own curved roof that extended over the previous floor. Around this magnificence, there were smaller buildings of similar design set in ornamental gardens and ponds. Lok didn't know it, but it would have pleased him to know that the picture was the home of a Japanese emperor.

Before it was half built, there were questions as to how he could afford to build such a colossal building. People came to stare at the extravagance, including Jenn and Keth. Immediately, Keth muttered, "It will not survive!" and when pressed to explain, he just repeated the statement. Jenn took him by the arm and led him away from the crowd.

"Is it something that you have seen with that object?" she asked him. Keth dumbly nodded and looked at the building with pain on his face.

A thorough investigation was launched into the finances of Lok Pren Enterprises, and the first thing discovered was that the records were a mess! Lok Pren was asked to explain, but he had gone up-country and could not be found. The remaining staff claimed that everything was handled by Pren and that they knew nothing about the finances. According to the papers so far discovered, Pren could not have built a henhouse let alone this monstrosity!

The engineers said that if the building was stopped, it would collapse, so it continued. The interior was a grand design and Pold and Gorb were contracted to do some of the less extravagant work. They entered the building and stood in stunned silence. They had the impression that the whole of New Town could have been contained within the mansion's walls.

It was when the council tried to look into Pren's past, that they found that he didn't exist! At that point, the task of building the structure was stopped; the structure was up and self-supporting so there was no danger.

The burning question was, 'Who was the real Lok Pren?' Someone had invented this person and built a complete legend, and then fabricated a growing business based on the fiction. The only photographs that could be found showed no facial features, not even a profile! At the address on the records, they found a confused old lady suffering from dementia; she was certainly no mastermind!

The attention of the investigation was changed to the companies that supplied Pren, and that was just as confusing; half of them did not exist! At least, when they checked on them, it was simply an address leading to another address and eventually they led back to Lok Pren Enterprises.

When the investigation had reached its fifth year, all trace of Lok Pren had vanished. For a real person that would have been difficult, but for a fictional character, it took just a moment. Instead, other companies popped out of nowhere that were run by more fictional characters. Was it one man, or a consortium of fraud artists?

What was more horrifying was that these new companies were destroying the ecosystem of the planet, and that was against the regulations; the lessons that had been learned from the abuse of the original home planet were being ignored!

As one company was closed down, another appeared in a different location. One of those companies appeared near the Grand Mansion, and very soon, the noise and pollution drew complaints and an official reaction.

For some reason that was not declared or understood, the company was drilling deep into the fabric of the mountain. The operation was stopped, and the residents sighed with relief. Two weeks later, their relief turned to horror as it was seen that the tall structure was leaning to one side. Day by day, the angle increased, and in the middle of the night, there was a tremendous thunder and shaking of the town. In the morning, the building could not be seen and when they arrived on the site, they found a large hole in the ground that descended out of sight. The Grand Mansion, surely a Folly in the true sense of the word, had been swallowed by the planet.

Aunt Middy had the last word, "Some wicked men had abused the planet, our home, and the planet has had its revenge!" She was talking to Father Chevens, who nodded sagely.

"We brought the disease with us; it lived on the ship for generations, hidden from sight and festering until this moment, it is called greed," the priest smiled, "Fortunately for us, this planet had the antidote!"

"You mean that the planet eats greed!" Aunt Middy said, and helped herself to another glass of her concoction. Father Chevens politely declined.

KID'S STUFF

Seg Ich stood higher than most in the community, at least head and shoulders higher! He looked more like a skinny caricature than a human being, long thin arms and legs that matched the long sorrowful face, a doodle on a school book. Also as the headmaster of the only school in New Town, in fact, the only teacher, he was held in high esteem. With the assistance of almost humanoid robots, he managed to produce some bright young minds.

On every morning from Monday to Friday, at the hour of nine, streams of children converged on the central school-house, like an army of chattering ants drawn to sugar. Seg stood at the door, towering over the children, and counted the heads as they passed him; with his remarkable memory, he knew who was going to be late or missing. There was never one to mention.

There were no partitions for the classes; even Seg's office was open to the rest of the school, not that he sat there most of the time, usually, he could be seen folding his long legs to bring him down to the same level as the student and they would discuss some subject until the student and Seg were happy with the result. He did this with all of the different age groups.

Nobody would say that Seg was an affectionate person; with his long sad face and deep voice, he looked more like an undertaker than a teacher. But the smile came readily, a transformation to humour, a laughing matchstick man. When the discussions were over, he would ruffle the student's hair with his long thin fingers and leave them glowing and confident.

As the school closed in the afternoon, the chattering ants would reverse the flow and go home. As the night closed over the clapboard schoolhouse, Seg would close down the automatons, switch off the lights, and go for his supper.

Tired children would sleepily yawn, stretch, and make their way to the bedrooms, pull up the covers and dream. After a while, Seg would also lay in his bed and dream, and he directed the dreams of others on adventures of what they had said in the schoolroom; together, they sank beneath the foaming seas and talked to the fish and octopus, played tag with the dolphins and sharks. The huge whale took them into the dark depths where unnamed creatures lived.

Others drifted high above the mountains and savannas to watch large herds of bison trek across continents. They soared with the eagle and condor, listening to their ancient cries. Others went further; they scooped up handfuls of moon dust and see it float in the airless space. They looked into the building of stars, to see the first glittering of energy.

The most senior students observed the appearance of life and how it evolved into more complex creatures; the different evolutionary paths that lead away from the others, and how some flourished and others died. They saw that the whole universe was an evolutionary event, and tried to understand how it started.

Non-students, parents and grandparents, were caught up in the dream-worlds and followed the history of the long voyage, and then the almost mythical history of the home-world. It was difficult for them because this was their home-world and the other was too distant in time and space, more dreamlike, full of fables and paradox.

The following day, the students, just like the sugar hunting ants, trailed noisily to school. They talked about their dreams and Seg would explain; he introduced the idea of graphs, geometry, and mathematics, leading them towards the science of everything. He did this with games and puzzles.

He also showed them how easy it was to ruin everything, and so difficult to build and make. That is what happened on the home-world, they ruined things to make other things, destroying life and creation until nothing was left. The values of the old world were false gods.

When many years had passed, Seg shed his mortal coil, that spidery frame that amused so many people. At first, people wept and mourned, but by the end of a week, their faces were brighter than ever, their laughter echoed in the Blue Mountains.

Every night, they would rush to their beds, and join Seg on a new adventure. There was so much to know, so much to learn, and Seg continued to lead them to new and richer lives.

REMNANT

In a place faraway by many aeons and by many parsecs, there was a solar flash; a blink of light that was so small compared to the immensity of space that it went almost unnoticed. It was the last gasp of an ancient star that had burned all of the elements that had given it life and the planets to which it gave birth.

On one of those planets, life had stopped long ago; the inhabitants that had stayed behind had long since passed onto a different type of world, a different type of life, at least it is hoped so. The husk of a dried world had circled the star many times without any creature on its surface; it was unable to sustain life; the huge generator in its interior had stopped producing energy, and the now poisonous atmosphere and oceans had dissipated into the vacuum.

Rocks that were even older than the star started to rain down on the surface, making craters in the endless desert, new mountain ranges that no one would ever climb. As the star came to the end of its fuel, it expanded into a huge red giant, swallowing half of its children, including the dried husk. And then the star contracted to become smaller than the planet.

The light went out.

ABOUT THE AUTHOR

Mike Williamson lives a few miles from Cambridge, UK, a wondrous place for anyone who is curious, and he is curious! The village he lives in can boast of an ancient church dating back to 900 AD, during the times of the Anglo-Saxons. This means that he is surrounded by science and history, and not surprisingly, these are among his interests.

From a very early age, he has been fascinated by science fiction and he has a collection of SF books that he reads over and over again.

He did not really start writing his own books until he took an early retirement, and it was an article about solar flares that led to his first book, 'Apollo's Fury', and the others followed on from there.

There is a touch of Irish in Mike, and he likes nonsense and fun of the type found in 'Alice in Wonderland', and if you read it carefully, it is not that nonsensical. In his early teens he found a book on a London stall 'The Silver Locusts', and he was captivated by the vision and language of Ray Bradbury. The book is better known as 'The Martian Chronicles', since the book was filmed.

To date, 2017, Mike has self-published 14 books, some of just short stories which pleases the busy people that read them. This book is the forth in a collection of short stories, and his 'fans' reach as far as Australia, the USA, and naturally Europe.

Printed in Great Britain
by Amazon

78556948R00055